Dozens of Dachshunds

A Counting, Woofing, Wagging Book

Stephanie Calmenson

illustrated by Zoe Persico

BLOOMSBURY
CHILDREN'S BOOKS
NEW YORK LONDON OXFORD NEW DELHI SYDNEY

To Mark . . . and to Harry —S. C.

To Lucky the Labradoodle. I am so "lucky" to have
grown up with a good boy like you. —Z. P.

BLOOMSBURY CHILDREN'S BOOKS
Bloomsbury Publishing Inc., part of Bloomsbury Publishing Plc
1385 Broadway, New York, NY 10018

BLOOMSBURY, BLOOMSBURY CHILDREN'S BOOKS, and the Diana logo are trademarks of Bloomsbury Publishing Plc

First published in the United States of America in June 2021
by Bloomsbury Children's Books

Bloomsbury books may be purchased for business or promotional use. For information on bulk
purchases please contact Macmillan Corporate and Premium Sales Department at specialmarkets@macmillan.com

Library of Congress Cataloging-in-Publication Data
Names: Calmenson, Stephanie, author. | Persico, Zoe, illustrator.
Title: Dozens of dachshunds : a counting, woofing, wagging book / by Stephanie Calmenson ; illustrated by Zoe Persico.
Description: New York : Bloomsbury Children's Books, 2021.
Summary: A galore of Dachshunds dressed in clever costumes gather in the park to celebrate Dachshund Day.
Identifiers: LCCN 2020028853 (print) | LCCN 2020028854 (e-book)
ISBN 978-1-5476-0222-3 (hardcover) • ISBN 978-1-5476-0223-0 (e-book) • ISBN 978-1-5476-0224-7 (e-PDF)
Subjects: CYAC: Stories in rhyme. | Dachshunds—Fiction. | Dogs—Fiction. | Costume—Fiction. | Counting.
Classification: LCC PZ8.3.C13 Do 2021 (print) | LCC PZ8.3.C13 (e-book) | DDC [E]—dc23
LC record available at https://lccn.loc.gov/2020028853

The art for this book was created digitally using custom brushes in Photoshop
Typeset in Brandon Grotesque
Book design by Danielle Ceccolini
Printed in China by Leo Paper Products, Heshan, Guangdong
2 4 6 8 10 9 7 5 3 1

To find out more about our authors and books visit www.bloomsbury.com and sign up for our newsletters.

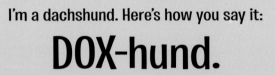

I'm a dachshund. Here's how you say it:

DOX-hund.

The dachshunds are coming! They're on their way.
Where will they go on this glorious day?

One dashing dachshund strolls down the street.
He's all dressed up for the friends he'll meet.

Two cheery dachshunds are out to have fun.
Each looks delicious in a hot dog bun.

Three dazzling dachshunds are feeling quite merry.
They're a trio of treats with whipped cream and a cherry.

Four royal dachshunds left their castles behind
to see what exciting adventures they'd find.

GO DACHSHUNDS!

Five feathered dachshunds wish they could fly.
They'd go soaring and gliding across the sky.

Six stripy dachshunds are covered in fuzz.
They bark their hellos. (Wait—shouldn't they buzz?)

Seven clever dachshunds are perfectly dressed
for sharing the books they each like the best.

Eight stylish dachshunds sashay through the city.
In all kinds of hats, they're so handsome and pretty.

Nine sporty dachshunds perk up their ears,
to hear their fans' whistles and rousing cheers.

Ten super dachshunds, fearless and brave,
look high and look low for someone to save.

Eleven woofing dachshunds pretend to roar.
It's fun to make noise like a dinosaur.

Roar!

Roar!

Twelve racing dachshunds go galloping past.
Giddy-up! Giddy-up! They move so fast!

Dozens of dachshunds begin to bark.
They know what will happen inside the park.

It's Dachshund Day, a day to have fun!
Everyone's here, and the party's begun.

The crowd starts singing the Dachshund Song,
with seventy-eight dachshunds barking along.

We love dachshunds, short and long.
They are bold, and they are strong.
They are loyal. They are proud.
They may be small, but their barks are LOUD!

Now the dachshunds are leaving. They're back on their way.
They had a great time on this glorious day.

We Love Dachshunds!

Dachshunds are long and low, but high in spirit.
All around the world, they are celebrated in festivals just like the one in this book.
Dachshunds have been painted, sculpted, photographed, and written about by famous artists and writers.
There is even a dachshund museum in Germany filled with thousands of dachshund objects.
These winners, wieners, and wonders are greatly loved by many people. That's worth barking about!

Dachshunds have three types of coats:

Smooth   Longhaired   Wirehaired

They come in different sizes:

Standard   Miniature   Rabbit or Kaninchen

Standard and Miniature are the most widely recognized.

There are many combinations of colors:

Black and Tan

Wild Boar

Chocolate and Tan

Wheaton

Chocolate and Cream

Red

Blue and Cream

Isabella (Fawn) and Tan

And several patterns:

Sable

Dapple

Brindle

Piebald

And more!

MEET A DACHSHUND

Photo © by Carmen Gonzalez Photography

Harry is a longhaired, chocolate-dappled, tweenie-size dachshund.

That's a l-o-n-g sentence for a short dog.

Harry lives with Stephanie Calmenson, who wrote this book.

He's been to the New York City dachshund festival many times.

Harry is very sweet. Sometimes, he is very loud.

When he barks, cover your ears!